# ONE IN A HUNDRED

# ONE IN A HUNDRED

CATHY THOMPSON

I dedicate this book to my Mom, Dad and my Lord,
whose guidance and unconditional love,
has enabled me to endure all that life has
bestowed upon me.

# PREFACE

Being blessed with a loving family was my inspiration for writing this book. Though it is categorized fiction, I did drift back in time and used a few memorable moments from my childhood. With so many miles now between us, I have adopted many friends, whom I consider part of my family as well. I have written this book as a tribute to my dear family and friends, whom I hold close to my heart. I would like each of you to know how important you are to me and how blessed I am to have all of you in my life. Thank you for all the wonderful memories.

Your daughter, granddaughter,
sister, aunt, niece, mema,
mom and friend, Cathy

# CHAPTER 1

Hank Thompson sat in his study like he did every morning, with intent to accomplish anything that would satisfy his desire to aid others. He had clearly reached a point in his life, where money was no object. He knew he was one of the wealthiest men in the world. He had made his fortune by making a few sporadic decisions in the past decade. Penny stocks had paid off for him. He would like to think it was wise decisions on his part and not pure luck. None the less, he took a few chances and with the help of a few clever investments, had managed to become one of the wealthiest of the wealthy. Among his many assets on display, were controlling interest in many major companies around the world, several vacation homes, a private jet, a yacht, in which he had named after his wife, and worldly paintings from some of the most renowned artist in history. The list goes on and on. His assets could be filed under each letter of the alphabet.

He had a lovely wife, Danell, and a healthy and happy six year old son, Leighton. He didn't have a care in the world. He could sleep all day if he wanted, but he didn't. His days were like clockwork.

He rose with the chickens. He would stop by the kitchen just long enough to grab his first cup of coffee. From there he would head to his favorite room in his 32,000 square foot mansion, the study, close the door behind him, and then turn on the television to listen in on the first news of the day. He would then stroll over to his 18th century, historic desk and more days than not, attempt to work on something that would or could change the course of some needy soul's life. He was a self made billionaire. Not just a millionaire, but a billionaire. He had a heart as big as anyone. As far as he was concerned, one of his objectives in life was to make as many worthy people just a tad bit more comfortable.

His dad had retired an executive from one of the more successful railroads. While growing up, his family was abundantly blessed with more than most families, but a well-structured and simplified lifestyle had always been what he was accustomed to. With two older sisters, most of his time was spent pursuing practical jokes and trying to escape the punishment of his deeds. He was raised in an era in which 5:00 p.m. meant everyone gathered around the table to have supper and share their daily experiences with one another. He grew up in a neighborhood where the kids played outside until dark then were called inside to get their baths. The remainder of the evening was spent in front of the television with the family and enjoying a night time snack before bedtime. No one knew the importance of a loving and shielding family better than he. The two most important things in his life were his wife and son, and he had no intention of changing that.

When Leighton had vacation time from school, the three of them would decide where to spend it. Every now and then, other family members would accompany them on their trips. Both Hank and Danell, tried to the best of their ability, to provide a loving and caring atmosphere for their son. Despite their fortune, they strived to maintain a simple and stable lifestyle. Hank and Danell had agreed never to let money go to their heads. Money was only an object. Family on the other hand, was true security.

Suddenly, there was a knock on the door of his study. Hank already knew who this was; the only person who seemed to respect his privacy, Ramona, the housekeeper. Ramona was a lovely, German lady in her 40's, very poised and proper. She wore her long brown hair in a ponytail, which was Leighton's fancy. He loved pulling on it and running away, as if, to provoke her to chase him.

Ramona knew when it was time for Hank's second cup of coffee, and would always bring it to him around 7:00 a.m. every morning, while he enjoyed his solitude in his study. She was enchanted by the study and enjoyed every encounter with it. She had one true passion and that was reading. The study encased hundreds of books, all of which had been read at least once, and sought after memorabilia was displayed throughout. Many times, Hank would ask her to choose a book. He knew she took as good a care of his books as he did and always returned them in a timely manner, placing them back in the exact spots she had removed them from. She was allowed in the study once a week to clean, and every morning around 7:00 a.m. in which to bring him his second cup of coffee. This morning she chose not to borrow a book. They engaged in usual exchanges of morning greetings. She removed his first cup of coffee from the coaster on his desk and replaced it with the fresh cup she had just brought him. With that done, she left the study to head off to another room in the ever so grand manor, which needed her proficient attention.

An hour had passed when the door to the study sprung open. Hank's meditation welcomed the sound of little feet making their way to his side. "Daddy, it's a letter for you," Leighton said, almost breathless, handing him the letter. Hank reached out and stroked Leighton's head, taking the letter. "No school for you today, hu? That's right, it's Saturday. Where's mom?" he asked. "Making breakfast," Leighton replied. "Good, I'm a bit hungry. How 'bout you? Let's see who this is from," he said, glaring at the envelope. After opening the letter, Hank immediately knew what this was in lieu of.

# CHAPTER 2

**1 1/2 Years Earlier**

It was a rainy, dismal, Saturday morning. Hank, sitting in his study, had almost finished his second cup of coffee, when Leighton entered like he did every Saturday morning, to get reacquainted with his dad first thing in the morning. They would exchange their hugs and kisses and interact in small talk. This particular morning, Leighton said something that was unfamiliar and a little startling to Hank. "What are you doing, daddy?" Hank had never had to share his thoughts with his son before now; grown-up thoughts; the things he thought about the majority of time spent in his study. "Well Leighton, I have been trying to come up with a way I could help people who are less fortunate than ourselves. You see, there are a lot of people in the world, whose life could be made a little better, if they just had a little more money. Since we have so much, I was thinking we could give them some. This way, their life could perhaps become a little better." Although Hank had always been a charitable man, it just never seemed like he could do enough for others in need to satisfy his good heartedness. He tried to explain it so a child, not quite 5 years, could understand. Leighton quickly replied, "Why don't you send one hundred people a dollar?" Leighton had no concept of money. He knew he had a piggy bank sitting on his dresser drawers that had money in it. Every now and then, his mom or dad would give him a few coins and encourage him to put them in his bank to save for a toy. Neither Hank nor Danell, believed in spoiling their only child. They intended for his life to be as normal and routine as any other child his age, without the entire getup that usually accompanies having riches. "Leighton," replied Hank, "one dollar would not be very helpful. A dollar does not go very far this day and age, I'm afraid." He saw the disappointment in Leighton's eyes. "I'll tell you what, I'll think about it. Okay?" Leighton ran over to one section of books.

These were Leighton's books. Danell had arranged them on a lower shelf so Leighton could reach them. Every evening before bed time, Leighton would choose a book for his dad to read to him. "Which book are you going to read to me tonight, daddy?" Leighton asked. "Whichever one, you pick for me to read," Hank said, knowing this was a difficult decision for Leighton to make at times.

Although it was raining outside, there was always plenty to do inside. "Let's play hide and seek, daddy," Leighton said, in that tone he used when he was excited about something. "Alright. I'll hide and you find me," Hank said, knowing full well, this was not how they played this little game that Leighton loved so much. "No, I get to hide," Leighton said, in almost a wine. "Alright. Go hide and I'll count to fifty," Hank said, closing his eyes while starting the count. This game came with two rules; no going outside, and no hiding upstairs. The house was much too large, to look everywhere, to find someone. Hank remembered one time Leighton had hid underneath the sink in an upstairs bathroom and fallen asleep. It took over an hour for anyone to find him. The entire household was in a panic, thinking he may have wondered outside and gotten lost, or in trouble somehow. The rules quickly changed from that time on. After searching and finding Leighton inside a linen closet, they heard the breakfast bell. Both looked at each other and simultaneously said, "time for breakfast."

For the next few days, Hank thought long and hard about what Leighton had said about sending one hundred people a dollar. Perhaps this could lead him into finding others that did need his help. The more he thought about it, the more in favorable he became of this idea. After all, Danell would often say, 'from the mouth of babes, comes many wonderful adventures', and after all, what harm could it do.

# CHAPTER 3

It was Tuesday morning. Danell was cooking breakfast and trying to get Leighton ready for his little people school, as Hank called it. Ramona had already brought him his second cup of coffee. Hank had been thinking for days about what Leighton had said to him. He finally had the notion to act out this almost senseless endeavor. Reaching in his desk drawer, he pulled out a few pieces of monogrammed stationary he'd had much too long, and laid them on the desk in front of him. He was about to embark on an adventure that he actually felt excited about. He then reached for a pen. It had to be black ink he thought. He preferred black over blue ink. With pen in hand, he began writing. 'To whom it may concern'; he frustratedly scratched that out and then decided not to begin with a heading at all. Just the letter itself would accomplish what he had set out to say. After he was finished writing, he sat back in his favorite, most comfortable, leather chair and read aloud what he had just written. *"Please let me introduce myself. My name is Hank Thompson. You do not know me, nor do I know you. As you may be wondering why I have sent you this dollar, let me reassure you, I too, find myself a little bewildered at this action. Please put the dollar away and spend it only as your heart leads you to. Perhaps one day, we will both know the purpose of this small and seemingly, insane gesture. Sincerely, Hank Thompson."* He then walked over to his copier and made 100 copies of the letter. He walked over to a file cabinet in one corner of the study and carefully counted out one hundred envelopes. It had been awhile since he had last opened the file cabinet. It had once belonged to his great, great grandfather. It always seemed out of place in his study but he felt fortunate to have such an old, worn out, heirloom that had been passed down for generations. Danell had at one time painted it, hoping to bring out some character to its unsightly beauty. Though Hank did not particularly care for the color she chose, he was not about to argue his wife's judgment, for she had quite a bark when it came to the decorating department in all their homes. He carefully folded each letter and placed one folded letter inside each envelope. All he had to do now was select the one hundred people to send them to, and place a dollar bill inside each. He would save these steps for a later time.

He was feeling hungry and knew breakfast would soon be ready. Hank left his study with intent to come back and finish this task as soon as possible. He entered the kitchen finding his wife and Ramona setting breakfast on the table. "Good morning darling," he said, while leaning to kiss his wife. "Are you hungry?" she asked. "I'm starving," he replied, smiling. Leighton ran into the kitchen, hugging first his mom, then his dad, and then Ramona, chattering the whole time. Hank closed his eyes for a second and with a very low voice said, "thank you dear Lord, for all the blessings you have bestowed upon me." Although they didn't belong to a church, Hank's belief in God was never denied. Hank felt his relationship with the Lord was as strong as anyone's. He loved the Lord and spoke to him regularly. God had always been a part of his life, and throughout his childhood, had many times witnessed God's presence. He had once told a room full of people, about the time his grandfather and he, were walking down a road, when suddenly, a car drove by and happened to hit a bee flying in its path. His grandfather got down on his knees next to the bee and told Hank to do the same. Hank could clearly see the bee was dead; its insides were even visible. Hanks grandfather told him to start praying for God to heal the bee. Both Hank and his grandfather started praying for God to heal the bee. Hank saw the bee fly away. He knew that bee was dead. He knew God had healed it. He knew the power of prayer. He knew the power of God.

After breakfast, Hank went upstairs to get ready to take Leighton to his little people school. Taking Leighton to school was something he enjoyed doing. It gave him a chance to have some one on one time with Leighton outside the home. He would often point out the different land marks along the way and read the street signs aloud to him. Hank considered this as much a learning experience as anything else Leighton would be taught in school. He would take different routes during the week. Each one would allow for visual variety along the fifteen to twenty minute drive. He pulled up in front of the school. Leighton unbuckled his car seat while Hank got out of the car and walked around the other side to let Leighton out. Hank and Leighton always walked hand in hand to his class room, and then Hank would give Leighton a big hug and turn to leave. He would usually walk a few steps away, and then Leighton would run to him, and give him one more hug before entering his classroom.

On the way back home, Hank thought about the note he had written and what the people might think, after opening their letter. He tried to remember word for word what he had written. Reciting it in his head, he debated on rewording it. He would have to reread it when he got back home, he thought. Maybe he would rewrite it. He was still having second thoughts about even sending it off. Then he said aloud, "yes, I will go through with this; no second thoughts about it."

Hank arrived back home and found Danell working in one of the flower beds. This particular flower bed was Danell's favorite.

There were many beds randomly arranged throughout the property, but Danell showed more attention to this one. It contained a few, small, flowering trees, along with several varieties of flowering plants. There was a bird bath in the center of it, and a few, small lawn statues scattered throughout. Hank's favorite statue was of a small girl, holding her dress up to just under her eyes. Danell named this one 'Miss Bashful'.

Harry had been their gardener for many years. Danell had a special fondness for him, probably because Harry always did everything to the tee, in which Danell asked of him. However, Harry had bad knees. He had difficulty stooping down to pull weeds. Danell, who loved working in the yard, made pulling weeds her responsibility. It gave her a chance to admire all the flowers and shrubs at an up close perspective.

Hank sat down in a chaise lounge near her. It was warm in the sun, so he decided to enjoy the warmth for awhile. He loved the outdoors, but had no desire to interfere with its natural course. He could be just as happy, embracing nature's undisturbed beauty. Danell, on the other hand, enjoyed a beautifully, well maintained and landscaped lawn. She knew as much about plant life, as any scholar horticulturist. Hank was always mesmerized over the aftermath, of an outside project Danell and Harry worked hard on. "Honey, I'll be in the study if you need me," he said to Danell, as he got up and headed back inside.

He opened the door to his study. He stood there for a second, scanning the room. The air always smelled especially pleasant inside the study. Danell used a special blend of Potpourri to fragrance the house. The scent was more noticeable to him, after the study had been shut up for awhile. He closed the door and walked over to his desk. He logged on to his computer and actually found it quite easy to retrieve an address directory from every state. He randomly selected at least one, sometimes two listings, from each directory.

He then, carefully studied each name and address as he wrote it on an envelope. He did this until all one hundred envelopes were completed. He then, opened one of his desk drawers and removed a role of stamps, placing a stamp on each envelope. It took more time than he had presumed it would. He knew nothing about the individuals, only that they resided in different regions and surely came from different walks of life.

After he was finished, he sat for a lengthy period of time staring at the one hundred envelopes, each containing the same letter. He reached inside one of the envelopes and removed the note inside.

He reread it to himself, folded it back up, and then placed it back inside the envelope he had removed it from. He was satisfied with what he had written. Nothing needed to be changed or reworded, he thought. Since this was Leighton's ingenious idea, he would let Leighton participate by putting the dollar inside each envelope. Hank looked at the lower right corner of his computer to check the time. He had to pick up Leighton from school soon. If he was to stop by the bank first, he had better leave now, he thought. He then left his study, closing the door firmly behind him.

On his way to pick up Leighton from school, Hank stopped by the bank to withdraw one hundred dollars from his checking account. There were very few customers inside, and that he was glad of. Maybe, he could get in and out of the bank as quickly as possible. He probably should have picked up Leighton first, but didn't feel like taking Leighton with him to the bank. Anytime Leighton was inside the bank with him, it seemed double the time was spent inside than would have been otherwise. He always dreaded going to the bank. He always felt all eyes were on him, whether they were or not.

He walked up to Genene. She was the teller who assisted him most of the time. He preferred her over the rest, because she was proficient and never tried to coax conversation out of him. "Hello,

Mr. Thompson. How can I help you today?" She always seemed to remember his name. This made him feel good. "Hi Genene," he went on, "I need to make a withdrawal from my checking account. I need a hundred dollars in one dollar bills, please." Without hesitating, she made a slip for him to sign and carefully counted back one hundred dollars to him. She didn't question his need for such a transaction and he was glad of that because he didn't feel the need to explain, nor did he want to. After bidding farewell, he started out the door. He was seen by the vice president of the bank, who instantly turned and gave his undivided attention to Hank. After a handshake and a few words of exchange, he was out the door and on his way to pick up Leighton from school. All in all, he was glad this stop took very little of his time.

Leighton's school only lasted four hours. Usually, Leighton was one of the first children picked up at the end of the school day. The classroom was still full of kids by the time either Danell or Hank picked him up. Today, he found himself running a little later than usual and called to tell Samantha, Leighton's teacher, he was on his way. When he entered the classroom, he noticed Leighton was the only child still inside. "I'm sorry I'm running late. Time seemed to slip by too quickly today." Today was the first time, in a long time, he actually had things to do, and he liked it. Samantha was not only Leighton's teacher, but also a very close friend; more Danell's friend than Hank's. Both Samantha and Danell had gone to school together and had remained close friends, even after both had set their sites on marriage and a family. "Tell Danell I said hello and I'll call her in a few days," Samantha said. "Will do. See you later. Sorry again," Hank said, on the way out of the room with Leighton at his side.

On the way home, Hank told Leighton about his day. He told him about the envelopes and the dollar he needed him to put inside each one, after they got home. "After all, Leighton," he said, "this was your idea and I think you should help me with it." He knew Leighton would be excited to help. "Yeah, sure daddy. I'll help,"

Leighton said. They were both excited about this whole adventure. Hank was excited about being excited. He was not one to sit at home all day with nothing to do. He enjoyed projects. It had been quite some time since he'd had a project to keep himself busy. He looked over at Leighton and smiled a big smile. They laughed and talked about nothing important, all the way home. Leighton was happy and Hank was happy.

# CHAPTER 4

After Leighton and Hank arrived back home, Leighton followed his dad into the study. Hank sat down at his desk and pulled out the bank envelope which contained one hundred dollar bills. Removing the dollars, he said, "Leighton, take one dollar and put it inside each envelope." Leighton did just as he was told. Hank watched as Leighton placed a bill inside each envelope. He then, carefully sealed each one as Leighton handed it back to him. The envelopes were finally completed. Now they had to be mailed. Leighton started toward the door of the study. Hank knew what Leighton's intent was, and said, "your mom's probably still outside working in the gardens."

Hank too, left the study, making his way from room to room, looking for Ramona. He found her in one of the family rooms dusting. "Ramona, I have several piles of letters on my desk that need to be mailed." He knew she would attend to this matter as soon as he had said it. "Should I gather them up and take them to the post office, Mr. Thompson?" she asked. Hank thought about it for a second. This seemed too important of a task for anyone but him to carry out. He should be the one to complete this important mission. "Second thought, I will take them to the post office myself," he said, turning to leave.

Hank went back to his study. He opened a lower drawer of his desk, and pulled out a leather briefcase Danell had given him a few years earlier for Christmas. He absolutely loved everything about it; the smell, the feel, the weight and color. He was glad it could be used for such an important matter. This was the first time he'd had the chance to use it. After opening it, he realized this was only the second time he had ever looked inside. It was quite handsome inside, as well as out. It was lined with brown and gold silk. He began placing the envelopes one at a time inside, while carefully reading aloud each name and address. He knew nothing about the individuals. Again, he wondered what their first response would be after opening their letters. After the last envelope was placed inside, he shut it and left it on the desk. He then left his study to look for Danell and Leighton.

He found them both in the kitchen preparing lunch. Leighton had snack time at school, but lunch was usually made soon after he got home. "Today's selection," Danell said, "is choice of two; egg salad sandwich, or BLT." Hank loved them both. "What are you having, Leighton?" Hank asked. "BLT," Leighton replied. "Alrighty then. Make that two, please," Hank said, looking at Danell and winking.

While all three were at the table eating lunch, Danell asked, "why don't we go out on the boat next weekend if it's not rainy?" The yacht was Hank's favorite pastime enjoyment. "That sounds like a wonderful idea," Hank said, looking over at Leighton. "Yeah, can we?" Leighton asked. "I don't see why not," Hank replied, feeling every bit as excited as Leighton. Hank knew all he had to do was tell Ramona of their plans and she would make all the calls and arrangements concerning the trip. Every time a trip was planned, the pilot had to be called. If the yacht was to be used, the captain had to be notified.

The yacht was a beautiful, two hundred foot cruiser, which Hank had found in Florence, Alabama several years earlier. Both,

Hank and Danell had fallen in love with it the moment they laid eyes on it. Hank renamed it 'Lady D', after Danell. They were so awed with the area, they decided to keep it docked there. Florence was a small town. Most, whom lived in the community, were born and raised there. Though Hank, Danell and Leighton were outsiders, they were treated like they too, had lived there all their lives. This was one of the most beautiful and hospitable places to be found anywhere.

A local man in the area, Jacob, was recommended to do all repairs on the engines. He also had a navigator's license. Anytime the boat was going to be used, he had to be notified so his schedule could be freed up in order to accommodate Hank. They all three loved going out on the boat. It had been a few months since they had used it. They all were ecstatic over the idea of spending time on the 'Lady D'. It was always nice when they got to plan a getaway. Vacation time, even if it was only for a weekend, was something everyone looked forward to.

After lunch, Hank knew he'd better go ahead and mail off the envelopes, before he changed his mind about the whole thing. "Leighton, I need to go to the post office to mail off those envelopes.

Do you want to go with me?" Hank asked, hoping Leighton would say yes. "Sure daddy," Leighton replied. "Go find your mom. Tell her we'll be back in a few minutes." Leighton, though only four years old, could be trusted to carry out most tasks asked of him. After doing what his dad had asked, he ran back to the front door of the house and waited patiently for his dad.

On the way to the post office, they discussed much about the upcoming trip. Hank knew Leighton loved going out and spending the night on the 'Lady D'. Just being out in the open waters, with nothing around but water and stars, was heaven on earth to Hank. He knew Danell and Leighton felt the same. The first night Hank had ever spent on the 'Lady D', he had stayed up all night, laying on the upper deck, looking up at all the stars and watching the reflecting lights dancing on the water. He had never been filled with such peace and tranquility.

Inside the post office, Hank laid the briefcase on the counter. He removed all one hundred envelopes, silently reading some of the names written on them. The postal worker fumbled through each one glancing to make sure each one had an appropriate address and stamp. Hank carefully watched as they were placed in a mail cart. Hank was starting to have mixed feelings about this. With his briefcase in one hand, and Leighton's hand in the other, he turned and walked away. It was done. It had been well over a year since Hank had partaken in any kind of work. He considered this to be work.

Whatever it was, it had a start, and it had a finish. He and Leighton had done it together, and that made him feel good.

# CHAPTER 5

On the drive back home, Hank thought about how he would tell Danell, what he had done. He usually didn't keep secrets from her. Normally, he would involve, and welcome her opinion on any proposal he took an interest; but, this time was different. He was actually telling her about it, instead of, involving her. He had been smitten by the idea of involving himself in the personal lives of others, with the intent, of a little good possibly coming from it, and had considered the possibility, Danell might disagree and discourage him from going through with it.

He remembered the first time he had ever met Danell. He was driving his dad's car in a neighborhood he had once lived in with his family. Danell still lived in the neighborhood. She was driving down the opposite side of the road and turned her car in front of his, forcing him to stop. At the time, she had thought it was a friend, whom had the same color car and looked identical to the one Hank was driving. She became embarrassed when she saw it wasn't who she thought it was, and started apologizing to Hank.

Before they drove off, Hank asked her if he could call her sometime. She gave him her phone number, and they started dating from then on. Danell was the most popular person in her neighborhood. She was the best dancer of anyone around. She was beautiful, charming, outgoing, and just a genuinely good person. Hank was lucky to have been blessed with such a gifted and wonderful wife. She was truly the backbone of this family.

His thoughts were soon interrupted by the sound of silence, and realized that Leighton had fallen asleep. How serene it is to be able to fall asleep to something as trivial as a car ride, he thought. For a minute, he thought about life itself. The first second of life is the easiest anyone will ever experience, and with the continuous passing of time, such is life's increase in difficulty, until death overcomes the mind and body.

"Wake up little buddy," Hank said, shaking Leighton's leg, to awaken him from his short nap. "We're home. It's time to get out of the car. Let's go find your mom." Hank helped unbuckle Leighton. They both walked inside the house. "Mama," Leighton started yelling. They found Danell outside enjoying a glass of sweet tea, looking over the yard, all the while admiring the beauty of the landscape. "In another month, it should be warm enough to start swimming in the pool," she said. "What have the two of you been up to?" she asked. "Just doing guy things," Hank replied. He knew this would probably be the time to tell her about the letters. He pulled up a chair and sat at the patio table with her. "We just got back from the post office. We had to mail something; something important." Hank was not going to let her get a word in yet. "Leighton came up with an idea about a week ago. I found it interesting actually, and decided to take his idea to heart, and did just what he had said for me to do. You know how I'm always trying to figure out a way to help people who may need help financially? Well, Leighton had suggested to me, to send one hundred people a dollar. Whether he had any idea of what he had even said, I have no idea. I just know, I told him I would think about it, and decided that maybe, that wouldn't be such a bad idea. So I wrote a note, randomly chose one hundred people to send it to, along with a single dollar bill enclosed, and Leighton and I took them to the post office and mailed off all one hundred of them." Here it comes, he thought; the scornful tone you would expect to hear when a child has done something so totally bad, that even, the good fairy could not possibly remedy it. He knew that look, and the words to follow would be those only one would say, when a dog has just soiled an Egyptian heirloom rug. Here it comes. He was ready. But, Danell merely shook her head in a positive manner, and with a soft spoken, calm voice, asked, "what?" Oh no, he realized he had to tell her all over again. This time he chose his words more clearly. "About a week ago, while I was in the study thinking about how I could help a few, needy individuals, Leighton gave me the idea of sending one hundred people a dollar. I wrote a note, and placed a copy of it, along with a single dollar, inside envelopes, in which I had randomly chosen one hundred people to send it to. I'll let you read the note later. It's in my desk. We just got back from mailing the envelopes," he said, in one breath. "I see. What do you hope to accomplish, or what do you think they will accomplish, with one dollar?" Danell asked. "Maybe, it will possibly lead me in the direction, of finding people who need a little financial help," Hank responded, not sure how well this was going. "I can't imagine what those people are going to think when they open their envelope and see one dollar inside it." Danell really didn't know what to think. She had never known Hank to do something of this nature before, and had never known him to do anything without her input. She was actually a little confused, and a little saddened that he had not told her about it until it was all over and done with.

All was quiet for a split second when suddenly Leighton said, "Can we get a dog? Kim has a dog." Oh, thank goodness, Hank thought. Many times before, Hank remembered how Leighton's little voice always sounded off at just the right time. Leighton couldn't have picked a better time to say something. Not only did it break the cold silence, it changed the subject about 360 degrees to the better. "Yes," said Hank while at the exact time, "No," said

Danell. Then Danell said, "Well, maybe we could think about it." "Isn't Kim one of your little friends from school?" asked Hank. "Yeah daddy, her dog's name is Bishop," Leighton said. "Well, that's a very nice name for a dog," said Hank. "Kim's parents got him from the animal shelter. She was telling me about him a few weeks ago when I picked Leighton up from school. Maybe, we could go to the shelter and look for a dog," said Danell.

Hank remembered he had left his briefcase in his car. He hoped he could quietly and quickly make his way back into the house without the envelopes being mentioned again. "Where are you going?" asked Danell. "That tea looks refreshing. I think I'll get some. Leighton, do you want some tea?" Hank asked, hoping he could just get back into the house without anymore mention of those envelopes. "Sure. I'll get it," Leighton replied, while running past Hank into the house. Hank was right behind him. He had made it. Maybe, just maybe, he thought, Danell would never mention the letters again. He knew one thing; he would never do anything like this again without telling her about it. He really didn't like to keep things from her. He knew how easily she got her feelings hurt. Not only that, she could make him start thinking twice about what he had done. He really didn't want to start wondering if he had done a very, silly thing. He hated more than anything to feel embarrassed. He felt vulnerable at this time and realized that he could start feeling embarrassed over what he had done if he didn't just stop thinking about it right now. He decided he would not think about those envelopes ever again, if possible.

# CHAPTER 6

It was Wednesday evening. All systems were set on go for the upcoming getaway. Ramona had taken care of all the arrangements concerning the weekend plans. Hank and Danell had decided to keep Leighton out of school Friday. This would allow for an extra long weekend to be spent on the 'Lady D'. Plans were, to pick up Leighton from school Thursday, head straight to the airport where their jet would be ready to whisk them off to Florence. There, a limousine would be waiting in ready mode, to transport them to the yacht.

Danell was upstairs gathering up any overlooked items of necessity she felt needed to accompany them on the trip. Hank and Leighton were in the study, bringing to close, yet another routine day. Leighton was trying to decide which book he wanted read to him before bed. Hank was swiveling in his leather chair contemplating the plane ride. His fear of flying was never far at rest in his mind. He hated flying. He usually made a stiff drink immediately after boarding the plane, hoping it would paralyze his brain just enough to keep his thoughts off crashing. Magazines and puzzle solving materials were scattered throughout the plane, so he could thumb through them in hopes of keeping his mind occupied on something other than the flight. Being a practical man, he knew he had no choice, but give in to the convenience of air travel at times. If he had any influence over economic structure, horse and buggy would still be the prominent way of travel in today's society.

"Leighton, haven't you decided on a book yet?" Hank asked. "This one daddy. I want you to read this one to me," Leighton said, rushing over to his dad, book in hand. Hank reached for the book. *"The Big, Yellow Plane;* wonderful," Hank mumbled; just what he needed to take his mind off flying. Sometimes, he wondered if Leighton had a sixth sense and enjoyed preying upon his weaknesses. Leighton climbed upon Hank's lap. After reading the book, Leighton climbed down and scurried over to put it back on the shelf; then walked back to Hank. They then, routinely bowed their heads in prayer. "God bless mama; God bless daddy; God bless Ramona, Harry, Gail, Diane, Kristen, Michael, Cain, Penny, Lisa, Teresa, Petri, Belvia and God bless me. Amen." Leighton recited his prayers every night before bedtime. This had been taught to him from the time he started speaking. "Amen," repeated Hank. "Off to bed, we have a busy day tomorrow. After school, we'll board the jet and be on the 'Lady D' before you know it." Leighton clapped his hands with excitement. After giving his dad a kiss goodnight, Leighton ran out the study. Hank walked over to the door, turned off the light, closed the door behind him, and proceeded upstairs to get ready for bed himself.

Upon entering the bedroom, Hank noticed Danell was still packing. "I'll pack my bag when I get back from dropping Leighton off at school tomorrow morning," Hank said. He was feeling much too tired to cram his brain with one more decision making activity today. For him, packing was merely a pick and choose saga anyway. He never spent too much time deciding on which outfits to take along. All the vacation sites were filled with closets full of appropriate clothing, no matter what the season or weather may entail. "I'm packing light. I know we'll only be gone a few days," Danell said. "I'm excited about the trip. It's been awhile since we've been on the boat," she added. "Yeah, I think we all are. I'm looking forward to another shrimp salad sandwich we get at that restaurant down from the boat," Hank said.

The *Seafood Palace* was a restaurant located around the bend from where the 'Lady D' was docked. Its' owners, Arnie and Rebecca, had used their life savings to buy the old, run down building. It had previously been a bait and tackle shop. They had turned it into the only fine dining restaurant in town. Fresh seafood and Prime Rib were its specialties. Hank more times than any, indulged on the shrimp salad sandwiches. Apparently Arnie had added his secret seasoning to the recipe and no one, but no one, could make it tastier.

"You know Hank, if you stay up all night tonight, maybe you'll be able to sleep on the plane tomorrow," Danell said, knowing Hank's weakness of flying. "I doubt it. You wanna here something funny? Leighton picked out 'The *Big, Yellow Plane',* for me to read tonight," Hank said, chuckling and shaking his head. "Well, you make it no secret, especially while on the plane, of your fear of flying. Every time we're in flight, you practically get sick. You start making everyone around you a little jumpy and anxious as well," Danell said. She too, didn't care too much for flying, but no one was as fearful of it as Hank.

# CHAPTER 7

Thursday morning arrived a little overcast. The first thing Hank did after entering his study, was zero in on the weather channel. Just by the look of it, he could tell rain may be in the forecast. This could mean the trip needed to be postponed. Flying in perfect weather conditions was one thing; flying in rain, however, put more stress on the already horrifying situation to commence. Hank had been known to cancel flights if just one raindrop was predicted. Perfect weather conditions had to be in order throughout the entire flight pattern in order for him to board a plane. He, like anyone else, knew his limitation. He was not perfect. Flying wasn't the only thing on his 'not to do list'; public speaking was certainly not part of his flair either. He could easily avoid speeches; flying, on the other hand, was inevitable.

The forecast showed twenty five percent early morning showers, clearer as the day went on. This eased his mind. No rain showed up on any satellites from noon on. The trip would be on schedule as planned. He sat at his desk and staring in space, asked God to provide a safe and pleasant trip for his family and him.

The knock on the door meant Ramona was outside with his second cup of coffee. "Come in Ramona," Hank said, while glancing at his cup of coffee in front of him. He had only drunk half of it at this point. Normally, he would be finishing it up by the time he got his second cup. None the less, it was no longer as hot as he liked it. "Ramona, are you sure you don't want to go with us on this trip?" he asked. "No sir. I think I'll go spend some time with my family. I should be back home before ya'll get back though," Ramona said, exchanging his coffee cup for the fresh cup she had just brought him.

Ramona came from a large family. She was never denied any request to visit with her family. Hank, Danell, Leighton and Harry, were like family to her as well. She had been Hank and Danell's housekeeper even before Leighton was born. Her immediate family lived within a fifty mile radius of her. However, like Harry, she too had her own room in the eight bedroom fortress. Her bedroom was set up like Harry's. They both resembled an efficiency apartment; each equipped with a luxurious bath and a roomy living area, along with an area just large enough for a bistro table and chairs inside a small, but functional kitchenette. It was like having a home within a home. Their rooms were located in the basement. They had a private entrance in the back. They could either enter their rooms through the rear of the house or through the front door. Most times they entered through the front door. At times, her family would visit her and every now and then one or two of her family members would spend the night with her. Hank and Danell were very lenient when it came to Ramona and Harry's family members visiting either of them. They often encouraged it.

Family and friends were always welcome. It made for a harmonious environment all around. 'Family and friends,' Hank often said, 'keeps the world afloat and sane.'

Hank turned off the television. While heading out the study, he thought about the letters. He had not had time to think about them for a few days. Surely, he thought, the people should have gotten them by now. Oh well, he was hungry and breakfast soon took over his immediate thoughts.

Hank entered the kitchen and to his surprise, noticed it was empty. 'What's this?' he thought. 'Danell's not in here cooking breakfast?' He opened the refrigerator, made a quick search of the contents and with disappointment closed it. Though he was a man of his own domain, when it came to meals, he could be classified more like a child forced to eat what has been set in front of him. He usually never took part in planning the daily feast and was always content with anything placed in front of him. He decided to go find Danell and without making it too obvious, beg for his breakfast.

He had no sooner turned around, when Danell and Leighton walked up behind him. "Hungry?" she asked. "Starving," was his reply. "I'm fixing corned beef hash and eggs this morning," she said, knowing that would meet his approval. "I made hash from the brisket we had the other day." She knew Hank always loved it when she took the leftovers and conjured up something tasty from them. Homemade corned beef hash was high on his list of desire, partly because Danell only cooked corned beef brisket a few times a year. Danell was a wonderful cook. She wallowed in the pleasure of seeing everyone's satisfaction over her worthwhile effort. "Why don't you go get dressed and I'll start breakfast?" she beckons, knowing he would have to drive Leighton to school shortly after breakfast.

After breakfast, Hank drove Leighton to school. On the way back home, he stopped by the bank to withdraw a little cash for the trip. When he arrived back home, he passed Harry outside pressure washing the circular drive. "Harry, don't forget we'll be leaving today when Leighton gets home," he said. Harry always chauffeured them to the airport. Hank rented a hanger at the airport where the jet was kept. The pilot, a longtime friend of Hank's, John William, took special care of overseeing the maintenance carried out involving the plane. John William had at one time been a partner of Hank's on a few real estate deals before he had run across some debt issues, thus proposing Hank to buy him out. They had remained close friends, and since John William was a skilled pilot, had graciously accepted the position as Hank and Danell's private pilot. Hank knew he could put his trust and faith in his friends' ability to maintain a safe plane and trusted his navigational skills to keep his family and him safe while in flight. Hank's problem of flying was due to uncontrolled thoughts of something beyond anyone's ability, happening to the plane while in flight. This was a phobia he felt would surely stay with him his entire life. He knew he had little choice but to grin and bear it when necessary.

Hank entered the house. Before going upstairs, he decided to check the forecast again. Nothing concerning the weather outlook had changed. He proceeded upstairs. He filled his carryon bag with items of importance and threw a few changes of clothes inside. He was done.

# CHAPTER 8

Hank could see the jet sitting on the tar mat from his window seat, inside the car. The door to the jet was open, and the steps leading down to the ground were awaiting its passengers. It was a beautiful jet equipped with modern technology. It had no history of system failure, no call backs from the factory, and no glitches of any kind. It was a magnificent aircraft with magnificent ability. It was not only beautiful, it was safe.

As Harry brought the car to a stop, Hank could see John William standing at the top of the steps. He made his way down the steps as everyone stood outside the car reaching for luggage. John William knew how bad Hank hated to fly. "Are we ready for this trip?" John William asked Hank, hoping to find his friend in a serene state. "Ready, as I'll ever be," replied Hank. "Doing alright?" Hank added. "Yeah; weather's clear; plane's good. I'm good," John William said.

"Harry, I'll call you Sunday to let you know what time to be back here to pick us up," Hank said. They shook hands. "I'll take care of the house. The flight will be okay sir. I'm sure." Even Harry knew what Hank was going through.

Two hours into flight, John William's voice came over the intercom. "We'll be landing in a few minutes. Everyone grab a seat and buckle up." Hank was always glad to hear these words. "Soon we'll be on the boat," Danell said. The excitement in her voice was obvious. She loved the yacht more than anyone. This was her yacht. The 'Lady D' was her, through and through.

John William had phoned the airport ahead of time checking on the limousine waiting to transport them to the yacht. Everyone exited the plane. "See you in a few days," Hank said, shaking the hand of his friend. "Have a good time," John William said. "Do you want to stay over on the boat with us?" Hank asked. "I need to get back. I'll see you in a few days." John William taxied the plane around and saw them off. He then took a spot at the end of the runway waiting to be signaled to take off again.

Everyone entered the limo. "Sir, could you stop at the closest grocery store on the way to the dock?" Danell asked the chauffeur. She had been writing a short grocery list while on the plane, and was scanning over it while in route.

No food was ever left on board the 'Lady D'. Enough items were brought on board to last through the stay and any remaining groceries were gathered up and given to the neighboring boaters before leaving the yacht. "Yes ma'am, there is one right up the road here," the driver replied.

The driver stopped in front of the grocery store. Hank, Danell and Leighton climbed out of the limo and raced toward the store. They all weaved in and out of the aisles, leaving Danell in charge of filling the grocery cart. Sandwich fixings, fruit, juice, milk, cereal, breakfast items and snacks were placed inside the cart. Dinner was usually eaten out, during their stay on the yacht, so breakfast, lunch items, and snacks, were all they really needed. Hank rarely went to the grocery store. Danell or Ramona did all the grocery shopping. Hank felt more like a kid in a candy store any time he was at a grocery store. Practically everything he saw, he wanted.

As the driver neared the dock all could see the 'Lady D'. She was the most beautiful and certainly the most enormous of all the boats docked. They could hardly wait for the limo to come to a stop so they could make their way to it. It was a beautiful, sunshiny day and everyone was eager to explore the area and greet other boaters they had not seen in a while.

All four climbed out of the limo. The chauffer helped carry the groceries down to the boat. "This is a fine boat you have here sir," he said to Hank. "We love spending time here on her," Hank said. "My name is Walter. When you get ready to leave here or if I can be of any service to you and your family during your stay here, please feel free to call me. This is my own limousine. I will be glad to take you anywhere you need to go, at any time," he added. Hank took his card and pulled out a folded stack of bills from his front pants pocket. He handed it to Walter. They shook hands then parted ways.

The boat appeared to be in the same condition, in which it had been left in, the last time it was used. Even though it had been closed up for several months, each room on the boat was equipped with its own air controlled ventilation system to keep mold and mildew out and to provide a well circulated airflow even though the boat remained unused. Hank made a quick sweep of the boat, inside and out, to insure no damage had been inflicted during storm activities that had occurred in the region since the last time they were on it. All appeared fine and Hank was ready to settle in and enjoy the view from the lower deck of the yacht.

Danell was still putting away groceries and packed items. Leighton was bouncing back and forth, from the deck to inside. Hank yelled to Danell, "I'm going to take a quick nap." He hadn't planned on it, but it was relaxing for him just sitting there with the soft breeze and sound of water echoing in his mind. All the sight, sound, and feel of the water lead up to one thing; a much needed nap. "Alright," she replied. "I'll keep an eye on Leighton." They were both very aware of Leighton's whereabouts when at the boat.

While Hank was sleeping, Leighton was inside his bedroom paying special attention to some toys he had not played with since the last time they were on the boat. Danell was making her way from room to room. The yacht was of such magnitude, once inside, it appeared to be a home one would find while looking through a *'Beautiful Home Magazine'*. It was designed so cleverly, that every inch of space had its own purpose. The long, white leather, wrap around sofa, not only contained unnoticeable storage units, but could double for more sleeping space. European tile was the flooring throughout. There was certainly no cost spared with the crafty, yet elegant design of this yacht. It contained a large master suite with an enormous bathroom, containing a full size shower and sunken tub; two other bedrooms, one in which contained a full size bath; a large guest bath with a sunken tub and separate shower decorated with inlaid Italian tile; a family room with a flat screen television; a den with yet another flat screen and dining table with chairs; a large eat in kitchen; a covered deck; an uncovered deck;

and an upper covered and open deck. The captains' quarters, just off the upper deck, was designed much like a studio apartment but on a smaller scale. The boat had once belonged to a CEO of an overseas corporation. It was only used as short time retreats for important cliental. It had not been used much when Hank and Danell bought it. During the first three months of ownership, they used it more than the previous owner had ever used it. During the summer months, much time was spent on the boat. Family often accompanied them. It was most definitely a favorite gathering spot for all.

Hank was awakened by the sound of the captain's voice. "I meant to be here when you arrived. Would you like for me to pull away from the dock now, sir?" he asked. "Danell is inside. If you would, please go ask her. It's fine with me," Hank replied, still sluggish and somewhat incoherent from his nap. He got up from his lounge chair and proceeded inside. The captain passed him making his way toward the upper deck where his room and the boat controls were located. "Jacob, everything okay with you? It's good to see you again," Hank said. Hank liked Jacob. He considered him 'just a good ole boy'.

Hank brought Leighton outside and together they climbed to the upper deck to watch as the captain pulled away from the dock and drove out toward open waters. Jacob drove it around for a few hours and then anchored it down. It was getting dusk. Danell had just finished whipping up a quick meal. She took Jacob a plate and returned inside. After dinner, Hank, Danell and Leighton returned to the top deck enjoying the sunset and skimming the water for a glimpse of marine life. Soon the stars would be all around them.

This seemed too perfect to be real, Hank thought, as he reclined back into a comfortable position to begin his lengthy gaze up at the stars. The weather was perfect. The sky was clear. He had no intent of leaving this spot for a while.

As he laid there staring into heaven, he thought about the envelopes again. None of them had been returned to him stamped, 'no longer at address', or anything to that matter. Everyone had gotten their letters by now. He wondered if anything would become of that well devised plan, which took so much consideration and thought.

"Are you about ready for bed?" Danell asked. "I'm going to give Leighton a bath and tuck him in for the night," she said. "I'll stay up here a little longer then I'll come inside," Hank replied. It was too surreal to end just yet, he thought.

# CHAPTER 9

It was Sunday. The weekend had passed too quickly. It was time to start thinking about the trip back home. After breakfast, Danell did some light cleaning and packing. Hank called John William after breakfast. He should be arriving at the airport around 3:00p.m. Hank called Walter giving him a time to pick them up. He would be there around 3:00p.m. If the jet was a little behind schedule, then it would allow for more time before they arrived at the airport. Hank called to the captain to start heading back to the dock. No one was looking forward to the trip ending except Leighton. He was anxious to get back home. Hank and Danell had promised him, after they returned home; they would all go to the local animal shelter and pick out a family dog. This would be the first time they had ever had a family pet. It was something each of them was looking forward to, especially Leighton.

After they arrived back to the dock, Danell took the unused groceries to the first boat owner she ran into on the dock. Walter arrived and helped load up the limousine. Hank left Jacob on the boat. Jacob always stayed behind to make sure the boat was secured and everything was turned off before leaving it. Hank had no sooner entered the limo when he started getting that paranoid feeling that always overcame him before he boarded the plane. Danell sensed it and said, "we'll be home before you know it."

The flight could not have ended any sooner. They were back on the ground making their way to the car. Harry had the trunk up and was heading in their direction to help them with their luggage. "Harry, I'm so glad to be back on the ground," Hank said, with much relief. "I know you are Mr. Thompson," said Harry. He knew as much as anyone about Hank's woe's. "You alright Harry?" Hank asked. "Good. You?" Harry asked. "I am now." Hank was relieved to be back on the ground.

Back home Ramona greeted them at the door. "How was your trip?" she asked. "I baked a ham if anyone is hungry," she added. They all left their bags sitting in the entrance foyer and headed toward the kitchen. All sat around the table eating and bragging on their weekend outings. It was always nice to return from an excursion but nicer just to settle back into routine, home life.

"We decided to get a family dog," Danell said. "Leighton has been whining for one ever since one of his little classmates got one," she added. "A dog around here may be fun for us all," Hank added. "I love dogs," Harry said, adjusting himself straight up in his chair. "I do too. I always grew up with dogs around," added Ramona. "Then it's settled. Tomorrow we'll go find a cute, little puppy for the family," said Danell.

After Hank unpacked his bag, he went to his study. He went through all the mail. He was particularly anxious to see if any response had come from anyone he had sent a letter to. A few magazines and a lot of junk mail were all he found. He stretched back in his chair and started thinking about how he could find people who needed his help. Maybe he could talk to the president of the bank tomorrow. He may know of some families that were recently turned down for loans, due to some technicality, that maybe, he may be able to help. He reached for a pen and on the memo in front of him, jotted down 'call bank president'.

The flight back home had taken its toll on him and he thought about taking a quick nap. He could go upstairs and lie down on the bed, find a chaise lounge outside and bask in the sounds of the outdoors, lie on the sofa in front of the television, or nap at his desk in his oversized, comfortable chair. All these had at one time or another welcomed his desire to doze.

"Daddy, it's time to read me a story," Leighton said, flying into the study. Hank opened his eyes. "What time is it?" he asked. "Almost bedtime," replied Leighton. "I must have fallen asleep. Pick out a book," Hank said, rubbing his face in his hands still trying to focus. Leighton handed him a book. Leighton climbed onto his lap. After the book was read, as Leighton was putting it back on the shelf, Hank said, "Tomorrow after school, Mom and I will take you to get a dog." Leighton was so excited, he started running for the door. "Get back here. Let's say your prayers," Hank demanded.

# CHAPTER 10

Hank awoke, grabbed a cup of coffee and made his way into his study. It was Monday. He turned on the television like he did every morning. Time to catch up on the news, he thought. He hadn't watched it since Thursday. As he sat down at his desk, he noticed the memo. He wasn't eager to talk with the bank president today. He wasn't one who enjoyed talking on the phone. He liked to say what he needed to say then hang up. He always found it hard to get off the phone with this man. He would rattle on and on about nothing and always seemed to pry in his business, which irritated Hank to no end. Hank wasn't a secretive man, but he didn't care to open up to people about his personal interest. He never pried into others' personal matters and he didn't like others prying into his.

The knock on the door signaled Ramona was on the other side with his coffee. "Come in Ramona." Hank welcomed the interruption. Not only was he ready for more coffee, he was distraught by the news he had been watching. "Why does it seem like the news is always bad things happening around the world, Ramona?" he asked. "Sometimes I wish there was a news channel to watch that reported only good things happening around the world," he added. "That would be nice, Mr. Thompson. Unfortunately, people love dirty laundry, as they say, and bad stuff is what people yearn to hear and read about." "You know, that gives me an idea. Maybe I will start a 'good news channel' and report only good things happening to people around the world. What do you think?" Normally when he said something, he was serious about it. Ramona looked at him and said, "Mr. Thompson, I think you can do whatever you set your mind to do. I have nothing but faith in you when you set your mind to something." She walked out of the room and closed the door behind her.

Hank wrote on the memo 'good news channel'. As he sat there thinking about the steps it would take to put something like this into operation, Leighton came running in. "Daddy, I get to get a dog today," Leighton said, running to his dad to hug him. "Morning Leighton. That's right, you do. After school we'll go get a dog. I bet there will be so many dogs to choose from it may be hard to decide." Hank had spent a good part of the morning wondering what kind of dog would be the best kind to have around Leighton. He had never seen Leighton interact with dogs and wondered just how rough he may be with one.

After breakfast, Hank drove Leighton to school. On the way back home Hank stopped by the bank. Genene was waiting on another customer. "Can I help you?" A woman approached him with her hand extended. "I'm Judy," she said as they stood there engaged in a hand shake. "I'm a new loan officer here," she continued. "Nice to meet you. I'm Hank Thompson. I don't have an appointment but I would like to see Jason if I could," Hank said. "Have a seat and I'll tell him you're here," she said, gesturing him to sit down in a nearby chair. Hank had only been sitting a few minutes when Jason, the bank president, came out of his office. "Hi, Mr. Thompson, please, come into my office," he said. "How can I help you today?" Jason seemed pleased to see him. "I've been feeling generous lately. I actually have been thinking about how I could help others who are less fortunate. As you may or may not know I support many charities. Many times I've discussed it with

Danell and we both feel the need to do more to help others who are in financial need. I suppose I could start right here in our own community. Do you know of anyone who may be down on their luck or who has been sticken with some misfortune that may need a helping hand?" Hank pleaded. Jason began telling Hank about a family who was about to loose their home due to some unusual circumstances. After what seemed like an hour, the meeting came to a close. With Hank's best interest at heart, Jason had persuaded Hank to open a separate account in which funds could be used for the mere purpose of helping others. Anytime Hank or Danell felt the impulse to help someone, the money could be taken straight out of that account. This account was to be used for people in distress right here in the community. Jason would call upon Hank or Danell anytime he knew of someone in financial distress and with either of their permission, the funds could be taken out of this new account to help those who needed it.

Hank left the bank feeling overwhelmingly righteous. So much thought and time had been spent contemplating ways to help people and now it seemed as if he would finally get his chance to make a difference in people's lives. He felt so blessed to have the life he had and now he could actually bring some relief to others in need of a little assistance. He knew Danell would be pleased. She had suggested to him the possibility that Jason may be able to help with this mission of theirs. After he arrived back home, he entered the house and to his surprise found Danell greeting him at the front door. "Guess what, honey?" Hank could hardly wait to tell her the good news. "I went to see Jason at the bank and he set up an account in our names that will be used strictly for helping people who need financial assistance; for instance if someone has been diagnosed with cancer and needs help with bills or someone is about to have their house repossessed because they are out of work and behind on payments," Hank said, before he was quickly interrupted. "I know all about the account. Jason phoned here saying you left the envelope on his desk containing the paperwork for the new account. He's going to mail it to us first thing in the morning. He's got the papers marked where I need to sign, also. I'm glad you went to him. This seems like a good way to help people right here in our own area." Danell was almost as excited as Hank. "I knew you'd be happy about it too," Hank said, while hugging Danell.

# CHAPTER 11

Hank stayed in the car while Danell went inside the school to get Leighton. As he sat there thoughts of a 'good news channel' engulfed him. He couldn't believe he was starting to think of this with some seriousness. He knew who he could take this idea to. He knew the local college had a media center. Sure, he had some influence with the college. After all, he had donated an acre of land several years earlier to the college where *Thompson Hall* now stood. He also had started a *Cap and Gown Fund* for graduating seniors who needed help purchasing not only their cap and gown but also their invitations for their graduation. Because of their generosity, Hank and Danell were always included in any functions thrown by the dean of the college; anything from dinners to balls. Just maybe he could have some influence with his idea. He could run this idea by Danell and make an appointment to see the dean in the near future.

He looked over to his right and saw Danell and Leighton approaching the car. Danell opened the back door to let Leighton in. Leighton climbed onto his car seat. "I'm going to have to take this out when we get back home and readjust the straps," she said, as she fought to buckle him in his car seat. "He's getting so big. I can hardly buckle him up in it now," she added. "Hey there buddy," Hank said, reaching behind the seat to make contact with Leighton's leg. "Next stop, Animal Shelter," Hank said, grinning to Leighton. "Can I get a dog today?" Leighton asked, in a voice with overwhelming excitement. "That's where we're heading now; to get a dog," Danell replied, with as much excitement as Leighton.

The three of them walked inside the animal shelter. "Hi. Welcome. My name is Marie. Can I help you?" the lady behind the desk asked, looking up from a pile of paper work she had been working on. "We were thinking about adopting a puppy," Danell said, positioning her sunglasses on top of her head allowing eye to eye contact. "We have quite a selection of puppies in our kennels awaiting adoption at the present. If you would like, I'll have one of the tech's walk you through. I bet you would love some of the puppies we have," she said, shifting her attention to Leighton. "That would be nice," said Danell. Marie picked up the phone, without entering any numbers, started talking to someone on the other end. Within a few minutes, a young lady entered the office. She introduced herself as Jessica and led them down a hallway. The first room they entered was lined with kennels on both sides. Each kennel contained at least one dog. Some contained as many as three. One kennel contained a mother dog with her pups. One dog started barking which seemed to encourage another and yet another until every dog seemed to be barking at them. One kennel had two small puppies inside. Leighton stopped in front of the cage staring down at them. "Last week someone brought in five dachshund puppies; three males and two females. All the males were adopted. These little sisters are still here with us. They are so sweet. They're seven weeks old," Jessica said, opening the cage. The puppies ran out jumping up on Leighton, Danell, Hank and making their way to Jessica as well. "Look how cute they are," said Danell. Hank picked one up. Danell picked the other up. Leighton started petting one, then the other. "Let's get both of them," Hank said, looking at Danell with a big smile on his face.

"Can we? Can we get both of 'em?" Leighton asked, looking at his mom then his dad. "Okay. Let's do. Want to?" Danell asked, looking at Hank. "Yeah, can we adopt both of 'em?" Hank asked, looking at the young lady. "I don't see why not," she said, taking both puppies and placing them back in the kennel. "I just need to get them ready. I need to check their charts and make sure they are up to date on shots and bathe them before I release them to you," she said, leading them out of the room, and back up the hallway into the front office. "Marie, they would like to adopt both the little, dachshund puppies. Marie will give you some paper work to fill out while I get the puppies ready," she said, leaving them up front to sign papers.

On the way back home, Danell held one of the puppies while Leighton held the other. "We need to think of some names for them," Hank said. "I want to name one Bishop," Leighton said. "That's your friend, Kim's dogs' name. It's a nice name for a boy dog, Leighton, but these are little, girl dogs and we need to think of girl names for them," Danell said. They all started babbling off names. Finally they all agreed on two names for their two, little girls. "Jenny and Jodie it will be then," said Danell.

After they arrived back home Jenny and Jodie were introduced to Ramona and Harry. Everyone took turns playing with the puppies and taking them outside. Danell and Ramona fixed a bed for them out of a box filled with old clothes. They were definitely welcomed members to the family.

# CHAPTER 12

Hank being the first one up in the house, checked on Jenny and Jodie before going downstairs to the kitchen. They were still asleep. He wanted to pick them up and nuzzle them but decided to let them sleep. He had to get that first cup of coffee down and put together some thoughts on paper concerning a 'good news channel'. After discussing it with Danell, he could get the ball rolling by calling the dean of the college. He wasn't sure how well this idea would go over with all concerned, but he did know that surely, he wasn't the only one who would like to watch good news for a change.

Hank was finishing his second cup of coffee and flipping through the channels when Danell entered the study. "Breakfast is almost ready," she said, while turning her attention to the television. "What's in the news today?" she asked, knowing he kept her up to date on any important happenings in the world. "Nothing good to report," he replied. "Honey," he went on, "I'm going to suggest to the college that they start a 'good news channel'. You know, there is a college broadcast channel on TV. It airs on a local channel. The media center at the college operates it, I'm sure. I was thinking about suggesting to them to add a 'good news' segment to it. I was thinking someone could start a web site that allows people from everywhere to write in and report any good news that has happened and the channel can broadcast the good news; a thirty minute segment entitled 'Good News'. What do you think?" Hank asked, awaiting a good response. "Actually, I really like that idea. The reason I don't watch the news anymore is because it's always so negative and depressing. That's a wonderful idea, Hank; you ready for breakfast?" she asked. Hank stood up from his chair and followed her out of the study talking about his idea all the while. "I'm going to call the dean today and ask for an appointment to talk with him about it. What's for breakfast?"

As they entered the kitchen, they saw Leighton lying on the floor playing with the puppies. "Should we take them outside to use the bathroom before we eat?" Hank asked, while stooping down to pat on them. "They just came in. They both used the bathroom outside. Maybe they'll be easy to train." Danell went on, "aren't they so cute?" "Getting the puppies was a good idea," said Ramona. "Leighton, leave them alone for now and get up to the table to eat," Danell said, while helping Leighton up off the floor. "You can play with them after breakfast."

After breakfast, Hank and Leighton took the puppies outside to get familiar with the outdoors. Hank sat and watched while Leighton ran around the back yard, puppies at his heels. Danell soon came out and joined in the play. "I'll be back in a minute. I'm going to call the dean," Hank shouted to Danell as he went back inside.

Hank returned outside. He was dressed in slacks and a collared shirt. "Going somewhere?" asked Danell. I've got an appointment with the dean in a few minutes to discuss that 'good news channel'. He can actually see me today. Wish me luck," he said, as he closed in on them. "You look nice. Good luck," Danell said. "Can I go daddy?" Leighton asked. "Not this time, Leighton. I've got a meeting with someone about a TV show, but I promise to tell you all about it when I get back home. Okay? Take good care of Jenny and Jodie and Mom while I'm gone," he added, while turning to walk back toward the house.

Hank arrived at the college feeling confident; a little nervous, but confident. As he made his way toward the dean's office, he rehearsed his planned outline of the idea. The first office he approached was the secretary's office. He introduced himself. Feeling this would take some time, he proceeded to sit in a chair. Before he had the chance to sit down completely, the secretary stood up and ushered him toward a closed door. "Hello Mr. Thompson. It's nice to see you again. I'm Mary, Mr. McCarthy's secretary. Mr. McCarthy has been expecting you." She opened the door and said, "Mr. McCarthy will see you now." Maybe this was for the best, Hank thought. Being rushed in to see him immediately, meant he didn't have to sit and wait with sweaty palms and second thoughts about his idea. He thanked the secretary, who shut the door behind him, and proceeded forward with his arm extended initiating a hand shake. The dean stood up from his chair extending his arm as well. "Hello Hank. I've been sitting here trying to remember the last time I saw you and Danell. I think it was opening night of the play, 'One To Live, Two To Die', a few months ago. How have you been?" "Very good, thanks. You?" "Actually, I haven't had that full of an agenda the last few weeks. Things have been running smoothly here, lately. Vallie should be here shortly. She's head of the Media Department. I wanted her in on the meeting as well, to get her input. I briefed her a little on the purpose of this meeting. I feel like you have a great idea. I'm all for a 'good news' segment, as well.

Actually, I can't believe it hasn't been suggested before now. How are Danell and Leighton?" "They're both fine, thanks. We adopted a couple of puppies yesterday. When I left the house, both Danell and Leighton were in the yard playing with them. We adopted them from the local animal shelter. Gosh, there are so many animals there. Its heart wrenching just to walk through and see them all," Hank said, thinking back on all the dogs they had seen while there.

A few minutes had passed when the door opened and a woman entered. She had a pleasant smile. Both men stood up greeting the newcomer into the room. "Hank, this is Vallie. She is the head of our Media Department here." "I recognize you from one of the charitable events my wife and I attended. Nice to meet you," Hank added.

The meeting lasted well over an hour. The dean looked at his watch and said, "I should be meeting Julie for lunch in a little while. Hank would you like to go with me? I'm sure she would love to see you again." "I need to be getting back to the house. Lunch is probably almost ready by now. I'll take a rain check though," Hank replied. "It has been a pleasure, Vallie," he said, as he stood up from his seat, shaking their hands, then turning to exit the office.

The meeting went very well, Hank thought as he headed toward the car. He could visualize the enactment of the 'good news' being reported as he headed back home. He realized just how hungry he was, and was looking forward to lunch. He could hardly wait to get back home and tell everyone about the meeting.

Hank arrived back home and found Danell and Leighton eating lunch. "We would have waited for you, but I wasn't sure how long you would be gone," Danell said. "Want some spaghetti?" she added. "I'd love some," he said, as he reached for a glass from the cabinet. As he stood pouring a glass of tea, he began telling Danell and Leighton about the meeting. "Vallie, with the help of some of her students, is going to set up a web site so people can post 'good news' stories. She said there will probably be so many posted that only a few will be broadcast; you know the best ones probably. Anyway, within the week, they will start building the web site. I can't believe how this just all fell into place like it did. I'm starving," he said, as he sat down and took his first bite. "We're glad it went well for you," Danell said, as she looked over toward

Leighton. "Are you going to be on television?" Leighton asked, taking another bite. "No, not me. Why, I would freeze up like a Popsicle if I was in front of cameras. Where are the puppies?" Hank asked, scanning over the floor for them. "Harry's got them outside. You ought to see him with them. It's so funny. He talks that baby talk to them. Well, we all do, I suppose. But, it just seems so funny hearing Harry do it," she said, laughing.

# CHAPTER 13

Days turned into weeks. Weeks turned into months. Fall had arrived. Most of the summer had been spent vacationing with family. Leighton was now six years old and attended first grade. Jenny and Jodie were no longer little puppies. They had grown up and though very similar for the most part, each had their distinctive personalities. The college station was set to air the 'good news' segment at 6:00p.m. today. Hank had been kept up to date with every detail concerning the progress and launch of the show.

It was Monday morning. Hank made his way with his first cup of coffee, like he did every morning, to his study. He turned on the television and sat down at his desk. Focusing on a small, framed picture, which for some time, rested on his desk, he reminisced the past. The picture was of Danell, Leighton and him sitting on the deck of the 'Lady D'. He thought back to that time and remembered it was a neighboring boater who had flashed their picture and had later given the photo to Danell. She had framed it and placed it on his desk. How slow time seems to go by at times, he thought, until one day you awaken and find time has slipped away. Time is the most powerful element of all. No amount of money or influence can control time. Dreaming would have to be second to time. Only in your dreams are you allowed to return back in time.

Hank was almost finished with his second cup of coffee when he arose from his desk and headed toward the kitchen. "I was just about to send Leighton after you. Breakfast is almost ready," Danell said. "You know what today is?" Hank asked, looking around the room at everyone. "The news comes on today," Leighton said, staring into his dad's eyes. "That's right, and I would like it if everyone would please adjust their schedule so we can all sit around the television together and watch it this evening," Hank said, drawing his attention to Harry and Ramona. "I wouldn't miss it for the world," Harry replied. "You know I'll definitely be watching it too," Ramona said. "As a matter of fact, I'll fix us a nice treat we can snack on while we wait for it to come on," Ramona added.

After breakfast, Hank walked Leighton to the end of the driveway and stood with him until the school bus arrived. Danell and Hank had decided Leighton would attend public school. Both private and public schools had their advantages and disadvantages. Kids would be kids no matter what atmosphere surrounded them. There were just as many, if not more, bad influential children, from well to do families, as there were from lower to middle class families. Both Hank and Danell had attended public schools and decided Leighton would do the same. This way he would get to know children from all walks of life and share in experiences he may miss out on if he attended a school that only upper class children resided in. Home schooling was definitely not an option.

This would be the same as removing Leighton from society and could result in long term effects concerning his social behavior. Being able to adjust well in society must be introduced to children at an early age. Being able to get along well with others and being outgoing should be instilled in all children. At least, this was the opinion of Hank and Danell.

As Hank and Leighton stood waiting on the bus, Hank quizzed Leighton on words that would be on his upcoming spelling test.

Apparently, Danell had spent time making sure he learned not only the spelling but also the definition. Leighton not only got all the spelling correct, but after spelling each word, correctly used the word in a sentence. "You are a very smart boy, Leighton." Praise was the best reward for any activity well done. Hank had been taught that as a child; just as you would praise a puppy for doing something good, it was just as important, if not more so, to praise a child for a job well done. Praise should be the reward for all good deeds.

# CHAPTER 14

Supper was prepared and eaten a little earlier than normal. Danell wanted to make sure the kitchen was cleaned up from supper and no one had anything that needed to be done as the time nearer the airing of the 'good news' segment. Ramona had prepared a strawberry short cake just for the occasion. As all was tending last minute activities, Hank moved to the family room, turned on the television, and set the channel to the college broadcast station. As he sat there, both Jennie and Jodie entered the room. Everyone came in behind them. Ramona and Danell brought in the sliced cake. Harry carried his piece and sat down in his usual spot. Ramona handed Hank his cake and grabbed her spot. Danell sat next to Leighton in her usual spot. Everyone had their own favorite seats. "Anyone want coffee?" Ramona asked. "I just made a fresh pot. I'm getting me a cup," she added. "Get me one too, please." Hank went on, "hurry, it'll be coming on soon."

The segment started with two college students sitting side by side at a counter like one would see during a regular, channeled, news report. "Hi, I'm Connie," said one of the students. "And, I'm Doris. This evening we will be introducing a new segment to our regularly broadcast show. A long time supporter and member of the community, Hank Thompson, approached the board of directors with an idea concerning a 'Good News' sector," said the other college student. "We are pleased to start the airing of that segment this evening. We would like to thank all involved in the outcome of this project. We would also, like to thank everyone who sent in 'good news' reports, which made it possible to launch our new segment. This time every evening we will be reporting on 'good news' happening not only around our community but also around the world. We have set up a web site, anyone can click on and post 'good news' happening around their community. We will select enough 'good news' every day to fill in our thirty minute segment. At the end of this program, we will give you the internet address to click on to, in order to post good news. And now for the 'good news' this evening …" Both students took turns speaking. As one finished, the other began.

*"Cranford and Opal in Oregon writes in … a fire engulfed and destroyed a three story, abandoned warehouse last night. Though thought to be abandoned, it was later determined it had been occupied by a mother dog and herjour puppies. The good news is, neither the mother dog, or any of her puppies were injured. They were all rescued by firemen at the scene. They have been adopted by the fire station and after the puppies are weaned from their mother, each puppy will be adopted by firemen and raised at home with his family, while the mother dog remains at the fire station as the mascot."*

*"Mikki in Michigan writes in … a commuter aircraft enabled engine problems while in route to Kalamazoo early this morning. The aircraft, with forty eight people on board, including five crew members, crashed into Lake Michigan. After spending several hours in the water, all aboard were rescued. The incident is being investigated. The good news is, not one passenger or crew member was injured."*

*"Troy in Florida writes in ... drought surely seemed the ruin of this small town, so a few local church members scheduled a prayer meeting in which the entire congregation gathered and prayed for rain. The next day it began raining. The good news is, it rained just enough to save all the crops in the area and bring the water level back up to its normal height for the census this time of year. "*

*"Chelsea in Georgia writes in ... a tornado swept through her small town of Lake Park yesterday evening. No injuries have been reported. One building was leveled as the tornado roared through town. The good news is, the building that was destroyed was scheduled to be torn down the next day by a demolition team." "Bruce in Chicago writes in ... his friend Katie had been in a coma from injuries sustained from a diving accident. This morning she suddenly sat up in bed and said, 'I'm hungry. I feel like I haven't eaten in days.' The good news is, after completion of medical tests, she was found to have nothing wrong with her and was released from the hospital, four months to the day she was first brought in."*

*"This bit of news comes to us from Germany. Ursula writes in ... while crocheting a blanket for her newborn grandson, a clap of thunder struck just outside the window she was sitting beside. The thunder was so loud, it shook the whole house. She could feel the house shake and saw the light from the lightning bolt. Immediately after that one, came several others. The first one she only felt and saw. The good news is, though she may not have been able to hear the first one, the bolts that followed she could hear, indeed. What was so amazing about being able to hear the ones that followed is that she had been born deaf. There is nothing wrong with her hearing now. People born with all five of their senses don't know just how lucky they are, she writes"*

*"And finally, some national news ... the center for Good Health and Disease has stumbled across a vaccine while performing tests in one of its laboratories. The vaccine has undergone a*

*series of protocols and has surpassed each one. A pharmaceutical company is in its final stages of completing the vaccine which will be released on the market very soon.*

*The good news is, this new vaccine is a cure for diabetes. This is a large step for the medical field. Millions of people around the globe are diagnosed with diabetes every day."*

*"This completes our first segment of 'Good News'. Remember to tune in every evening at 6:00p.m. to see what's good in the news. If you have any good news to report, you can visit our website at www.ihavegoodnews.net. Thank you for tuning in. Good night everyone."*

Everyone sat in silence for a few seconds. Leighton was the first one up. "I have to go to the bathroom," he said, heading out of the room. Hank pointed the remote control toward the television, turning it off. "That was good. I really enjoyed that." Everyone seemed to be voicing at the same time, their positive response to the show. Ramona and Harry left the room taking with them their empty plates that once displayed a perfect slice of strawberry shortcake. "The cake was delicious, Ramona," Danell said, holding her plate now empty, also. "It was good. I might get another piece, in fact," said Hank, also leaving the room. "I'll let the dogs outside," he added. As he left the room, he felt very pleased with the outcome of the program. It felt good to watch 'good news' being reported for a change. He was eager to congratulate everyone involved in this project. What a fine job had been done; a fine job indeed.

# CHAPTER 15

Hank stayed outside until Jenny and Jodie had finished their mission and was ready to come back inside. He inched his way to his study, peering in every room he passed, to account for everyone's whereabouts. As he made his way to his desk, he remembered the letters he had tucked away in one of the desk drawers. The latest one had arrived just a few days earlier. Danell had read them all. He was waiting for the right time to read them to Leighton. Leighton's mental capacity was developing at such a level, that he would soon be able to share them with him.

It was getting close to bedtime. Leighton opened the door to the study. Seeing his dad at his desk, he made his way over to his books. "Time to read me a bedtime story, daddy," he said. He reached for a book, sighted another, then another. "Leighton, bring me a book," Hank said, sitting back in his chair with his fingers locked behind his head. "I can't decide which book to get," he said, scanning the selection of books in front of him. "You know what, Leighton? I think I'll read something else to you tonight. Since you can't find a book for me to read, I've got something here in my desk I think you would like read better than a book, anyway. Come over here," Hank said, realizing this was probably the perfect time to introduce Leighton to these very important and cherished letters. "Get in my lap like you always do," Hank gestured, helping Leighton onto his lap.

Hank opened his top right desk drawer. While Leighton watched in silence, he pulled out a stack of opened letters. "I know you're wondering what these letters are. Do you remember when I wrote one hundred people and you put a dollar inside the envelopes? I know it's been a long time since we did that. Do you remember?" Hank asked, again. "Yes sir, I remember. We went to the post office and mailed them, too," Leighton said, shaking his head up and down. "That's right. I'm glad you remember. Well, what I have here is some responses to some of those letters. I actually have four letters here, which four people sent me, after they got their letter we sent them. They wrote back telling me what they did with the dollar you placed in each envelope. Do you want me to read to you what they wrote?" Hank knew what Leighton's response would be as he opened the first envelope to remove the letter inside. "Yeah, read 'em to me daddy," Leighton said, with overwhelming excitement. Hank very carefully unfolded the first of the four letters and glancing at Leighton, whose eyes were already fixed on the letter, began reading aloud.

*Dear Mr. Thompson,*

*My name is Steve. A little over a year ago, I received a letter from you with a single, one dollar bill inside. I have no idea if I was the only person you sent such a letter to, or if there are others. I never thought I would be writing you back regarding that letter and dollar. I searched high and low to find the envelope you sent them in. I am not a well-organized individual and could not remember where I had put it, or if I had even felt the impulse to save it. After a little searching, I found it tucked away inside a drawer of my dresser, letter still inside.*

*Getting to the point, I am writing to tell you, "Thank You". I feel as though you may be my guardian angel or something to that nature. At first, I thought you must be some kind of coo coo. I think otherwise now. You see, I tucked that dollar away in a fold in my wallet. I ended up spending it about two months ago.*

*One evening around 6:00p.m., I don't even remember what day it was, only that it was a week day, not a weekend,, a little neighbor girl, Brooke, came knocking at the door. Normally, one of my children would answer the door, but on this particular evening, I happened to be the one to go to the door. I remember it so vividly. She had a smudge of chocolate on her face. I told her she must have just finished eating a piece of chocolate cake. She said that she had. "How did you know?" she asked. "Because some of it is still on your face," I said, laughing. She was carrying a box. The lid was down on it so I couldn't tell what was inside. She carefully set the box down on my front porch just outside the threshold and opened the lid. Inside were two, eight week old kittens. She asked me if I wanted to buy one for a dollar. She had a cat named Spooky, who'd had six kittens. Her mother told her she had to try to find homes for them. She had two kittens left to find good homes for, she said. I, not being a cat person, had no use for one.*

*I can't tell you what made me change my mind. I found myself reaching in my wallet to give her a dollar and realized I had no money in there. I remembered the dollar you sent me which was tucked away in a tiny compartment and pulled it out. I actually remember saying to myself as I was handing Brooke the dollar, "This kitten must be special for me to be giving up this particular dollar for it."*

*One of the kittens was awake and one was sleeping. I chose the one that was asleep because I didn't want it to wake up and find itself alone. I called to the kids to come down stairs. I have three beautiful children; Maggie, Gracie, and Hunter. I showed them the kitten. Of course they were all excited. I, myself, was in a state of shock. I couldn't believe what I had just done. My wife, Abbey, heard all the commotion and approached us. She was as happy as the kids, upon seeing the kitten. At first they all debated on what to name it. They finally decided on Ashes. Ashes slept in the room with the girls.*

*Four nights ago I was awaken by Ashes. She had left the girls room and came into Abbey and my room. She had been purring at my face which woke me. Upon wakening, I petted on Ashes and got up and went down stairs to the kitchen to get a drink of water. It was almost 12:30a.m. The closer I got to the kitchen, the stronger the smell of smoke. I was fully awake by the time I reached the kitchen. I found the trash can on fire. It had just caught fire so it was easy for me to put out the flames. It must have been smoldering when Ashes first entered the bedroom and woke me up.*

*I can't help but think what the outcome could have been, if not for Ashes being here with us. The thought that I had used that single dollar from you to get her is still so overwhelming. I know nothing about you but just felt that I should write to you and let you know how I spent the dollar and again thank you.*

*Should I find myself on the receiving end of another dollar, I will not find it so weird the next time.*

*Thank you,*
*Steve & family*

Hank began folding the letter back up and reached for the envelope to put it in. "That was a nice letter, wasn't it?" he asked Leighton, as he reached for another letter. "Yes sir. Are you going to read another one?" Leighton asked, as he watched Hank take another letter out of another envelope. "Thought I would. You want me to, don't you?" Hank asked, while he carefully unfolded the second letter. "I want you to read all of them," Leighton replied, adjusting himself on Hank's lap. "Alright, here's another letter," Hank said, glancing over the letter.

*Dear Mr. Thompson,*

*I hope you remember me. I'm Cindy. Some time back, I received a letter from you with a dollar inside. I have enclosed a copy of the letter you sent me just to jolt your memory. I found it peculiar when I received it. No one I knew had gotten one, and I wondered, 'why me'?*

*Three months ago, my husband had back surgery. He still hasn't been able to return to work. We have four children; JR, Jennifer, Katie, and Caisey. Though I work full time, we were on the verge of losing our home and car. Our electricity had been cut off once, but I had that turned back on. What I'm trying to say, is that we were in financial ruin. Trying to work and care for a family all by myself, was not working for us.*

*A few weeks ago, my neighbor, Marjorie, called and invited me to go to the flea market with her. Knowing I had no money, I thought it would be good for me just to go along and get out of the house. I'm a server at a local restaurant, and believe it or not, I'm either at work or at home. I have no time or money to go or do anything. So I decided I would go along with her just for a change of scenery. I had no intention or money to buy anything.*

*It was actually fun walking around looking at all the different venders and their goods. One vender we came upon had a box of jewelry. I started going through it. It contained bracelets, rings, and necklaces. It was old, used jewelry. Everything in the box was just a dollar. I picked up one* necklace and studied it several times. I gave in to its charm and bought it. I was actually surprised to find the dollar you had sent me, still behind my driver's license inside my wallet.

Just last week, I was wearing the necklace while working. One of my customers commented on it and said I should have it appraised. I took it to an appraiser. It turned out to be a 17th century Victorian piece. The appraiser offered me $36,000.00for it. We paid off our car, caught up on bills, and were able to get eye glasses for our daughter, Jennifer. We also put away some in our savings account. I thank you. My husband thanks you. My children thank you.

If you ever happen to be in Valdosta, Georgia, maybe you can come by Willy's Restaurant where I work. The food is great. Also, I owe you a great, big hug.

Thanks again,
Cindy

*P.S.*
Dinner's on me!

"Wow! That was something. She bought a necklace with the dollar you put inside the envelope, and turned around and sold it for $36,000.00. That was a nice letter, wasn't it?" Hank asked, while folding the letter and placing it back inside the envelope he had removed it from. "Yes sir. Read the next one," Leighton said, anxious to hear the next letter. "Okay. Let's see what this person writes," said Hank, unfolding another letter.

*Dear Mr. Thompson,*

*My name is Web. With the help of my wife, Joyce, we are writing this letter to you on behalf of my mother, Ruby.*

*Over a year ago, my mother received a letter from you. Inside the letter you had enclosed a dollar. At the time, the dollar seemed of little significance. However, that dollar has since unfolded significant importance surrounding the event we are writing you about today.*

*Our family attends a small church on the outskirt of town. Our town is but a small farming town. One of the families of our church has been suffering for some time. Their youngest child has been diagnosed with chronic heart disease. The family spends more time in the hospital than they do at home The church members do what they can to help; from cooking meals to cutting their yard and cleaning their house.*

*Last week my mother brought the letter to church you had sent her. Before service started, she had a word with our preacher and left the envelope with him. At the end of the service, just before the offering plate was passed around, he read your letter and the dollar which had been tucked away in the envelope was placed in the plate. Everyone pulled out their wallets and checkbooks that morning. The money was given to the family.*

*In a few days, their child will undergo the operation she has so needed. Money will not be a factor in this delay any longer. Our entire congregation thanks you. Enclosed*

*You will find a picture of us all standing in front of our church. In the center, is our preacher, Casey. To his right, is his wife, Vivian and their son's, Herman and James. My mother, Ruby is pictured in the wheelchair. I'm standing beside her with my wife, Joyce. As you can see, we have just a small congregation. We would love for you to visit our church anytime. You will always be in our prayers.*

*Thank you,*
*From all of us*

"What do you think of that? That was a nice letter too," Hank said, folding the letter back up and inserting it back in its envelope. "That was a nice letter too, daddy. Read another one," Leighton said, picking up the last envelope. Hank took the envelope from Leighton and pulled out the letter which was neatly folded inside. He unfolded it. "Let's see what this person writes," he began.

*Dear Mr. Thompson,*

*After much thought, I have decided to write you this letter. A little over a year ago, I received an envelope in the mail. Inside I found a letter you had written, along with a dollar. I was a little disturbed while reading it. At the time, something told me to keep the envelope and letter. I'm glad I did.*

*My name is Jeena. I'm writing to tell you just how important that one dollar came to be. You see, when I was an infant of five months, my parents left me in the care of my Aunt BJ and Uncle Burt. My parents had to fly to Birmingham, Alabama on a business trip. They never returned. They were two of the victims on flight 123 which crashed into Logan Martin Lake. My aunt and uncle raised me along with their other children. I never knew my real parents. As far as I was concerned, my aunt and uncle were my parents. They loved and nurtured me as if I were born their own. I could not have possibly asked to be raised among a more loving and caring family.*

*I left home when I started college. After college, I accepted a job in Georgia. As with all children who grow up and leave home, there never seems to be enough time left for old friends and family.*

*My uncle died a sudden death four years ago. I never got to see him before he died. Three weeks ago, my aunt passed away. I was making the drive from Macon to Coosa Island. I was six miles away from the hospital my aunt was admitted to, when I ran over a bolt in the road and had to pull into a garage and have my tire replaced. I tried calling the hospital but my phone did not have a signal. Credit cards are my preference choice of payment for everything. Normally when I make a trip, I make sure I have some cash on me. However, I was in a hurry to see my aunt and decided not to go by the bank. If I needed anything, I assumed I could just use a credit card.*

*I noticed a phone booth outside the garage and remembered I still had the dollar you sent me. I exchanged* it for four quarters and was able to call my family who were in the room with my aunt. I was able to tell my aunt how much I loved her before she passed away. They had always told me how proud they were of me and I was given the chance to tell her how proud I was of them.

Last August I married a wonderful man, Casey Taylor. One day I hope to be a mom. I only hope I raise my children as well, and with as much love, as my mom and dad did.

I am an attorney in Macon. Should you ever need any legal assistance, please don't hesitate to ask.

Sincerely,
Jeena

P.S.
No charge.

"That was another wonderful letter, don't you think?" Hank asked, as he folded the letter back up and placed it back in the envelope. "Yes sir. Is that all?" Leighton asked, squirming to get down off Hank's lap. "Yep, that's all I've received so far. You never know, maybe more will come. Okay you. It's time for your prayers, then off to bed," Hank said, placing the four envelopes back inside the desk drawer.

After Leighton said his prayers, he kissed his dad goodnight, and left the study, closing the door behind him. Hank got up from his desk and started toward the door. He stopped a few steps from the door, turned around and walked back to his desk. As he stood behind his desk, he reached for a pen. In black ink, on the memo pad, he wrote, 'pick up one hundred dollar bills from bank'.